Little Cat's Luck

Also by Marion Dane Bauer

Little Dog, Lost

MARION DANE BAUER

Little Cat's Luck

illustrations by JENNIFER A. BELL

Simon & Schuster Books for Young Readers
New York London Toronto Sydney New Delhi

SIMON & SCHUSTER BOOKS FOR YOUNG READERS
An imprint of Simon & Schuster Children's Publishing Division
1230 Avenue of the Americas, New York, New York 10020

For information about special discounts for bulk purchases, please contact Simon & Schuster Special Sales at 1-866-506-1949 or business@simonandschuster.com.
The Simon & Schuster Speakers Bureau can bring authors to your live event. For more information or to book an event, contact the Simon & Schuster Speakers Bureau at 1-866-248-3049 or visit our website at www.simonspeakers.com.
Jacket design by Chloë Foglia, based on a design by Lauren Rille
Interior design by Hilary Zarycky
The text for this book was set in Perpetua.
The illustrations for this book were rendered in pencil and finished digitally.
Manufactured in the United States of America
0116 FFG
First Edition
10 9 8 7 6 5 4 3 2 1
Library of Congress Cataloging-in-Publication Data
Bauer, Marion Dane.
Little cat's luck / Marion Dane Bauer ; illustrated by Jennifer A. Bell. — 1st edition.
pages cm
Summary: A little cat named Patches manages to push out a window screen and leave her house, chasing a falling leaf, and sets out to find a special place to call her own.
ISBN 978-1-4814-2488-2 (hardcover) — ISBN 978-1-4814-2490-5 (eBook) [1. Novels in verse. 2. Cats—Fiction. 3. Adventure and adventurers—Fiction. 4. Dogs—Fiction. 5. Animals—Infancy—Fiction.] I. Bell, Jennifer (Jennifer A.), 1977– illustrator. II. Title.
PZ7.5.B385Lg 2016
[Fic]—dc23
2014037635

For Bailey Dane Bataille and Cullen Bauer-Trottier.

The wide, wide world is waiting.

—M. D. B.

Acknowledgments

My thanks, as always, to Rubin Pfeffer of RPContent, agent extraordinaire!

And to my editor, Kristin Ostby, who saw this little cat home.

Little Cat's Luck

1

Little cat,
searching.
Little calico cat
searching for a place,
a special place
to be her very own.

What she would do with a special place
once she found it,
she wasn't sure.
Perhaps she would just curl up for a good nap.

But if she didn't know
what her special place was for,
she knew exactly
what it would be like.
Hidden away,
snug,
dark,
quiet . . .
very, very quiet.

The little cat,
whose name was Patches,

by the way,
had checked
every possible spot
in her
entire
house,
looking for her special place.

Corners,
closets,
cupboards.
Even the dusty space
behind the refrigerator
and the floor beneath the kitchen table
next to the chipped blue bowl
that held her kibble . . .
and occasionally a touch of tuna.
Nothing
was quite right.
Not the pillow
where she slept
next to her girl's sweet breathing.
Too open.
Not the basement
where her man pounded nails
and whirled saws.

Too noisy.
Not the studio
where her woman
slathered paint.
Too smelly!

And so,
on the day our story begins,
Patches sat just inside the window
at the front of her house,
gazing out
at the wide wide world

and l o n g i n g.

She licked a paw
and ran it over her ginger ear.
She washed her black ear next.
But just as she was starting on
her pretty white face,
something caught her eye.

Something golden.

Something

f
a
l
l
i
n
g.

2

The golden leaf
wafted
this way
and that
as though it meant
to go anywhere
but
down.
"Come catch me!
I dare you!"
it seemed to say.

The white tip of Patches's patchy tail
twitched
and her eyes—
as golden as the leaf—
blazed.

"I want . . .
I want . . .
I want . . . ,"
she chirred.
And her wanting grew more fierce
with each saying of it.
So fierce that,
without thinking what she was doing,
she sprang
at the window screen
that stood between her
and
the
falling
leaf
and all the rest of the wide world.

To her astonishment
the screen gave way.

And Patches found herself standing
among the red berry bushes
that grew
around the base
of the house.

All this happened so fast
that the leaf
still floated in the air.

It twirled,
dipped,
drifted toward the grass,
and then . . .
just as Patches crouched,
ready to leap again,
another breeze tossed the leaf high.

She pounced and
missed.

The chase was on!

3

Across the lawn,
along the sidewalk,
  down
  the
  middle
  of
  the
  street,
Patches followed.
(Lucky there were no cars coming.)

She tiptoed
through more grass—
ew-w-w! prickly!—
then crossed a second street.

Still,
    the
        leaf
            called.

(Or perhaps
by this time
she followed a different leaf,

still gold,
still calling.)

Just when Patches
got close enough
to pounce,
another gust came along,
and the golden leaf

up
and
sailed up
and disappeared

of

peak a

the red

over roof.

The little cat slowed,

stopped,

sat.

She licked her nose.
(In case you didn't know,
that's what cats do
when they're upset.)

She wrapped her tail
around her haunches
and peered
over one shoulder.
Then the other.
But she could no longer
see the leaf
anywhere.
For that matter,
she could no longer
see her house
anywhere
either.

She was alone
under the blue bowl of the sky.

Now,
you might think a small cat,
a small *house* cat,
who has been petted and cuddled
and fed from a chipped blue bowl
her entire life,
would be frightened

to find herself alone
out in the BIG world.

But Patches hadn't forgotten
the important search she was on.
She looked around and thought,
Look at all this space!
There must be hundreds
of special places out here.
Thousands.
Each one more hidden away,
snug,
dark,
quiet,
than the one before.

What luck
that the golden leaf had called her!
What luck
that the screen had released her!
What luck
that the whole blue-and-gold world
l a y s t r e t c h e d o u t b e f o r e h e r !
What excellent luck!

4

Some cats
are born to adventure.
They prowl their towns
night and day,
exploring shrubs,
alleys,
the Dumpster
behind the butcher's shop.
They catch a mouse or two
and scatter
a flock of
sparrows.

Then they have
a howling fight
and,
pleased with themselves—
and perhaps a bit bloody—
they pad on home
to ask
politely
for a bit of cream.

As you already know,
Patches was not
one of those cats.

The closest
she had ever come to adventure
was the time,
this past summer,
when Thomas,
the orange tabby
who lived next door,
slipped through a gap
in the screen door
for a visit.

They had played
chase over the sofa,
    roll across the rug,
        hug under the table
the whole afternoon.
But the instant
Patches's family arrived home
and found Thomas visiting—
too soon,
too soon—
he had slipped away
through the same gap
that had let him in.
(Sadly,
the next day,
when Patches

checked out the screen door
herself,
she found it
sealed up
tight.
So Thomas never returned.)

But Patches's time with Thomas,
though certainly an adventure,
had taught her
little about the world.
The truth was,
she knew as much
about living outside
on her own
as you and I would know
about living
on the moon.

Still . . .
she swiped a paw across her whiskers—
a cat must always make sure
her whiskers
are clean
and in good order
before she takes on

any serious endeavor—
then she rose,
and,
holding her tail
  straight
    as
    a
    p
    o
    k
    e
    r,
she moved on.

If she went back home,
her family would,
no doubt,
fix the loose window screen
just as they had fixed the door.
So if there was ever a time
to find
her special place,
it was now.

A dog
barked in the distance.

Patches had never met a dog.
Not nose to nose,
anyway.
She'd seen lots of them
trotting by her watching window
on leashes.
They seemed
such foolishly obedient
creatures.
Still,
it might be interesting
to meet a dog.
At least it would be someone
to talk to.
Humans were so little use
when it came
to talking.
Or perhaps
it would be best to say
they were of so little use
when it came
to listening.
Mostly they did
all the talking
themselves,
as though

a perfectly intelligent cat
had nothing to say.

And who knew?
Dogs might not be as foolish
as they looked.
This one might even know
about special places.

No harm in asking,
anyway.

Patches set off
in the direction
of the noise.

5

Gus was the meanest dog in town.
Everyone said so.
He lived
in the green yard
belonging to a small tan house
on the corner
of Birch and Larpenter Streets.

The post office,
the Piggly Wiggly,
and Joe's Gas and Grill
sat on the other three corners,
which made Birch and Larpenter
a very busy intersection.
And that made Gus
a very busy dog.
All day

he up down
ran and
his chain-link fence,
barking at every car
that passed by.

He barked at every bicycle,
too.
In fact,
he barked at every cat
and dog
and person
who ran
or walked
or tried to sneak past.
Sometimes he even barked
at the birds
in the trees
just to show them
who was boss.
He curled his lips
to show his long yellow teeth
and growled
and snarled
and yelled.

"Go!
"Get out of here!
Go! Go! Go!"

Not that humans heard
"Go! Go! Go!"
They heard only

"Bark! Bark! Bark!"
But you and I know
what Gus was really saying.

Gus was enormous,
but he wasn't exactly handsome.
He had long legs
and a skinny tail
and ears that hung down
like limp
w
a
s
h
r
a
g
s.

He had a head
about the size
and the shape
of a shoe box.

He was gray,
the color of the ashes
left behind in your fireplace

after the cheerful fire
has grown cold.
And his coat was coarse
and wiry,
not the least bit soft
to the touch.

Gus wasn't an orphan.
He had a man,
a woman,
a boy
inside the tan house.
Actually,
he had once lived
inside the tan house
himself.
He'd spent his puppyhood
there,
cheerfully knocking over vases,
putting his paws
on the shoulders
of visiting grandmothers,
and gulping
every bit of food
he could get
his mouth

around.
And what Gus could manage
to fit into his enormous mouth
was truly amazing.
Once
he rested his chin
on the dining room table
and ate
a huge steak,
three baked potatoes,
a green salad,
and an ear of corn
without pausing
to take
a breath.
(It was when he stopped
to spit out the cob
that he got caught.)

And it didn't help
that when one of his humans said,
"Sit!"
Gus got a look in his eye
that said,
Who, me?
or that when they said,

"Stay!"
he galloped away
and
  ran
    all around
  the
house.

Then
there was that other problem.
I don't like to mention it,
but the truth was . . .
Gus smelled.
And when I say he smelled,
you will understand
he did not smell
like roses
or like baking bread
or like any of the many scents
we all welcome
when we walk
into a house.
He smelled—
no doubt about it!—
like dog,
a large

and rather dirty
dog.

And yes,
I hear your question.
"Hadn't anyone ever thought
of giving the poor thing
a bath?"

If only the problem
could be solved
so easily.

You see,
the man,
the woman,
and the boy
had tried,
more than once,
to bathe Gus.
But Gus was so big
and the tub so small
and the water so wet that . . .
well,
let me explain it this way.
Imagine the damage

an enormous dog
might do
galloping
merrily
through a small house.
Then consider
what an enormous, wet, muddy, soapy dog
might accomplish
careening
through the same small space.

So perhaps
when you consider all Gus's faults
you'll understand
why the man finally declared
that Gus must
never,
ever,
ever
come inside the house
again.
You might think the man hardhearted—
the boy did—
but even the woman agreed.
"Some dogs are not meant
for inside,"
she said.

Which was why Gus
lived in the green yard
and spent his days
running along the chain-link fence
shouting, "Go! Go! Go!"
It was also why
he'd turned
sad
and angry . . .
and,
let's face it,
rather mean.

Gus didn't mind
that the town thought he was mean.
In fact,
he had grown rather proud
of his fierce reputation.
Proud of the way
a dash at the fence
with his bark blaring
could make folks decide,
quite suddenly,
to cross   the street
(pretending
as they hurried away
that across the street

was where they had meant to go
all along).

And so,
when Gus saw
a small calico cat
marching toward him
with her tail high,
as though she owned the whole town,
he took his job
as the protector of his corner—
not to mention his reputation
as the meanest dog in town—
very seriously.
"Go!"
he shouted.
"Get away from here,
right now!
Go! Go! Go!"

The little cat
kept right on coming.

6

Gus couldn't believe his eyes.
Nobody
walked right up to his fence
that way.
Nobody in this whole town!

It didn't help
that the invading cat
had a helter-skelter look
about her.
One ear black,
the other ginger.
Black and ginger patches
tossed
        here,
there,
        and everywhere
on a white background.
Even her nose looked patched,
half pink,
half black.
Such a cat
shouldn't be taking herself
quite so seriously!

Gus tried again.
“Get out of my sight,
you ugly thing!”

If someone called you
an ugly thing,
you’d probably turn around
and leave.
I know I would.
But though Patches certainly heard—
Gus was so loud
she couldn’t help
but hear—
she
kept
on
coming.
Like every cat in the world,
she knew herself
to be beautiful,
so it never occurred to her
that Gus might be talking
to her.
And if she had realized,
she would simply

have decided
he was a very foolish dog.

Gus was so flabbergasted
that he swallowed
the rest of his barks
and stood staring
at the little cat.
Gazing into eyes
as golden as two small suns,
Gus found himself thinking,
just for an instant,
that he might have been mistaken
when he called this cat
ugly.
He didn't say that,
of course.
Who ever heard
of the meanest dog in town
apologizing?

Patches marched right up to the fence.
"I'm looking for a special place,"
she informed Gus.
"It has to be private—

very private—
snug,
dark,
quiet.
I want a place that—"
But by this time
Gus had overcome his astonishment.
He'd gotten past
admiring Patches's eyes,
as well.
And he opened his mouth
so wide that,
if it hadn't been for the fence
that stood between them,
he could have taken in
the whole
of the small calico cat
in
one
bite.

"GO AWAY!"
he roared.
"THIS INSTANT!"

Now,
Patches,
as you know,
was not a worldly cat,
but she wasn't a foolish one
either.
Without another word
about special places,
she turned around
and marched back across the street,
carrying her tail
tall
and
proud,
the
white
tip
flicking
with
each
step.

The flicking
of that white tail tip
enraged Gus.

Who was this patchy little cat
to make a fool of him?
How could she
walk up to *his* fence
and demand a special place
like that?
Even Gus's boy,
when he came into his yard
to bring fresh water
and kibble,
stepped carefully.
Quite respectfully,
really.
And no one—
no one!—
had ever walked away
from his fierce barking
quite so calmly
as this
small
cat.

Still . . .
what could a self-respecting dog do
except to say it all
again?

"Go!"
he shouted.
"Go! Go! Go!
And don't you
ever,
ever,
ever
come back!"

Patches did what she was told.
She kept going.

But as to never coming back . . .
well,
that was another matter
entirely.
Because while she'd been standing
close to the fence,
she had noticed something
very interesting:
two bowls
next to Gus's doghouse,
one filled with fresh water,
the other with kibble.
Patches had been well fed
that morning,

so she wasn't hungry yet.
But it occurred to her
that there probably wouldn't be
any chipped blue bowls
out here in the wide wide world,
so she made a mental note:
kibble and water
near the mean dog's house.
This
was a place
to remember.

After all,
the great noisy thing
had to sleep
sometime.

Didn't he?

7

The problem with searching
for a special place
without knowing
where such a place might be—
or even what

it might look like
should you find it—
is that the search
can take a great deal
of time.
And it did.
Patches wandered
from yard to yard,
from street to street,
from park to parking lot to downtown storefronts,
without once getting a glimpse
of the special place
she longed for.

Was it the sheltered spot
beneath the picnic table
in the park?

No.
Too many people
had gathered there
to eat lunch.

Was it the concrete urn
filled with flowers
on the steps of city hall?

No,
the urn had no roof.
What if it rained?
She glanced up
at the single dark cloud
c r a w l i n g
across the face of the sun
as
    it
        slid
            down
                the
                    afternoon
                        sky.

Was it the space
beneath the Dumpster
behind the butcher's shop?
No.
It smelled nasty.
But even the smell
of meat going rotten
made her tummy rumble
and reminded her
how late it was getting.
Almost dark.
Well past her suppertime.

And though Patches kept searching,
when she paused,
at last,
to look up at the star-pricked sky,
she found she felt
very
small,
just a bit lonely,
and
extremely hungry.

The little cat had searched so long,
in fact,
and grown so weary,
that she might have
given up entirely
and gone back home
to her girl.
If she had only known
where her home
and her girl
had gone off to!

But she had been walking
for so long
that she had quite forgotten
where she had come from.

So what could a small cat do
but keep walking?

She walked
until the pink-and-black pads
of her white paws
were sore.
And even then,
she walked some more.

Patches walked
until she found herself
on the corner
in front of the post office
once more
with its
f
l
a
p
p
i
n
g
red, white, and blue flag.

How could she have made a circle
without even knowing?
And there was that mean dog again,
barking.
"No! No! No!"
he was saying.
"Go! Go! Go!
Get away from here!
This corner is
mine,
mine,
mine!"

"Who wants your old corner?"
Patches said,
more to herself than to him.
But even as she said that,
she remembered . . .
fresh water
and a big
bowl
of
kibble!
Beside the doghouse!
And even as she was thinking

about water and kibble,
a drop of rain landed
right
on her small
pink-and-black
nose.

Patches looked around
for someplace dry.
Only the blue postbox
looked the least bit
friendly.
It stood up on legs
just the right height
to shelter a small cat.
Not the special place
she'd been looking for,
certainly,
but it would do
for now.
Perhaps someone had put
this blue box
here
just for her.

So Patches crawled
beneath the postbox

and lay down
out of reach
of the rain.
Her tummy rumbled,
reminding her
of what she'd known
for hours.
She was
very,
very
hungry.
She didn't know when
she'd ever been
quite so hungry.
Thirsty,
too.
She gave her grumbly tummy
a lick,
just so it would know
she still cared,

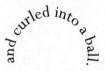

and curled into a ball.

There it went again,
that rumbling!
Her tummy rumbled so hard

that it wriggled,
too.

"Oh my,"
Patches said.
She'd never felt anything
quite like that
before.

All of which
made her think again
about the bowls
of food and water
beside the doghouse.
But Gus was still busy yelling,
"Go! Go! Go!
Get out of here!
Now!"
making it clear
that he wasn't asleep.
So she gave her sore paws
each a lick
and tucked her nose
beneath her tail.
Certainly *she* was sleepy

even if the dog wasn't.
So sleepy
that neither the rumbles
nor the wriggles
in her tummy
could keep her
from closing her golden eyes
and slipping
away.

First she dreamed
of her warm, comfortable house,
of her chipped blue bowl filled with kibble,
of her girl.

And then she dreamed
of her special place.
It was waiting for her.
Somewhere near.
She was certain of it.

8

When the mouseling
stepped on Patches's whisker,
the little cat woke
with a start.
It's odd,
as I'm sure you know,
for a mouse to walk right up to a cat
and step on her whisker.
But the night was dark,
and this particular mouse
was very young.
Also, he was excited,
which was why
he wasn't paying attention.
He'd been scurrying
home to his mother,
eager to show her
the bright red berry
he held
carefully
in his mouth.
In the darkness
he hadn't noticed
the crazy-quilt curl of fur

when he ran
beneath the postbox.
And it was just bad luck
that the whisker
lay in his path.

Have I mentioned Patches's whiskers
before?
Not just that she washed
and smoothed them
regularly,
but have I told you
how magnificent they were?
In case I haven't,

I'll tell you now.
Patches's whiskers were splendid.

White.
THICK!
L o n g !
Long enough
to be stepped upon
by a mouseling
so excited about
his red berry
that he forgot to look out
for obvious dangers
such as cats.

And that is how
Patches's whisker,
her very own l o n g, white whisker,
tugged her awake
from a sound sleep.
She jerked her head up,
slapped her paw down,
and caught
the mouseling
neatly

in the curve of her claws.
"Help!" he cried,
dropping the red berry.
"Let me go!"

Patches's tummy rumbled.
Every cat knows
that mice—
even little mouselings—
are good
for eating.
Patches had never actually
eaten a mouse.
In fact,
she had never even met one.
(I've told you she was not
a worldly cat.)
But she was pretty sure
this was
a mouse she held,
in the curve of her claws.
Still,
just to make sure
before taking a bite,

she asked,
"Who are you?"

"I'm a mouse,"
quavered the tiny fellow.

"I knew that,"
Patches snapped.
(She was usually
a polite cat,
but having to ask
something she should have known
rather embarrassed her,
so she covered her embarrassment,
as folks sometimes do,
with a sharp remark.)
"But,"
she added
in a more pleasant tone,
"surely you have a name."

By this time
the tiny mouse—
who,
though he was very young,
didn't have to ask any questions

to recognize a cat . . .
or the claws of a cat
holding him captive,
or the teeth of a cat
gleaming above him—
had begun trembling
from his teensy whiskers
all the way down to his skinny tail.
Still he answered bravely,
"I don't think I do,"
he said.
"Have a name,
I mean.
My mother calls me mouseling,
but she calls
my brothers and sisters
mouseling too.
So it's not quite the same."
And then he looked
into Patches's golden eyes
and said,
"I've heard
you have to own a human
to have a real name.
Do you own a human?"

"Of course,"
Patches answered,
her voice growing softer
at the mere mention of her humans.
"At least,
I had a girl once.
But a golden leaf
came dancing,
and she got lost."

(Cats,
as you may have noticed,
are not much inclined
to take responsibility
for their own mistakes.)

"Oh,"
said the mouseling.
He wasn't sure
he understood,
but it seemed best
to keep the cat talking.
Talking was far better
than biting,
chewing,
swallowing.

At least it was better
for him!
So he wriggled just a bit
to get away from the claw
pressing on his soft, round ear
and asked,
"Was she a nice girl?"

"Very nice!"
Patches said.
"Very, very nice!"
And then her tummy rumbled,
which reminded her that,
however nice her girl
might be,
her girl wasn't here now,
and that she,
Patches,
was very,
very
hungry.

Patches looked down at the mouseling
still held snugly
beneath her paw.
Where should she start?

With that funny little nose?
The whiskers might tickle.
With the skinny tail?
Certain to be rubbery.
Even while she considered,
her tummy rumbled again . . .
more loudly
this time.

"Please!"
whispered the mouseling.

And that's when Patches
realized her mistake.
Making conversation with your dinner
is *never*
a good idea.
It makes the first bite
so very
hard
to take.

"Please!"
the mouseling said again,
and his pink nose
with its tickly-looking whiskers

went
sniffle-sniffle-sniff.

Without another word,
Patches lifted her paw.

And the mouseling
snatched up his bright red berry
and
s
k
i
t
t
e
r
e
d
away.

Patches laid her white chin
on her white paws
and sighed.
What kind of a cat was she,
anyway,
who couldn't even eat a mouse?

Her tummy rumbled
more loudly than ever.
Then it wriggled again,
just for good measure.

9

When Patches woke again
night still lay heavily
upon the world.
Nothing stirred,
not even a mouseling.

She crawled out
from beneath the mailbox.
The rain had stopped,
but the sidewalk was still
unpleasantly wet.
Her tummy rumbled
and wriggled
even harder than before.
Patches stepped onto the grass.
It was wetter still.

If she were home,

she would be

curled on her girl's pillow.

Just thinking about
her girl
and that soft pillow
and the sweet smell
of her girl's breath
when she slept
almost set Patches to purring.
Almost.

She *wasn't* home,
though,
and her girl *wasn't* there,
so the purr got stuck in her throat
and stayed silent.
Patches looked up
at the fat-faced moon
peeking out
from behind
his cloud.
"Can you help?"
she asked.
"You must see everything

from up there.
I'll bet you know
all the special places.
I'll bet you even know
where my house is."

The moon said nothing.

"Please!"
said Patches,
remembering how
she seemed to have no choice
but to do what the mouseling asked
when he'd said, "Please."

"Please!"
she said again.
"Will you help me?"

A silvery voice
floated
down
from
overhead.
"What-what-what
are you do-doing down there

in the night?"
it said.
"Don't you know
everybody's
s-s-sleeping?"

The moon!
The moon had spoken . . .
and to her!
Patches was so excited
that
a
ridge
of
hair
stood
up
all
along
her
spine.

Still
she answered politely.
This was the moon
she was talking to,

after all.
"Dear sir,"
she said,
"I'm down here
in the night,
looking for a special place.
One of my very own.
And I'm lonesome
and damp
and much too hungry
to sleep."

"Oh my,"
said the moon.
"My-my-my!
I'm good at special p-p-places.
It's one of-of-of my specialties,
didn't you know?
And I'm g-g-good at hungry,
too.
Just-just-just you wait!"

So Patches did.
She sat down
in the wet
grass

and waited
for the moon to feed her.

In a moment
she heard a skittering
in a nearby tree.
The skittering
was followed
by a swish in the grass.

Was the moon going to come so close?
Patches had thought
such an important gentleman
would merely drop
something
from the sky.
A shower of kibble
or perhaps
a bit
of tuna.

She closed her eyes
against the shine
that was sure to come
and waited
some more.

When nothing happened,
she opened one eye.
Then the other.
The night was as dark
as before,
and the moon still floated
in the sky
far away.
But a small red squirrel
sat in front
of her,
holding a fat acorn
in her precise
little
paws.
"H-h-here it is!"
she said.
"Enjoy-joy-joy!"

10

"Oh!"
said Patches,
in a rather small voice.

When you're expecting the moon,
it can be hard
to know what to say
to a small red squirrel.
But still,
the little cat gathered herself
quickly.
She was,

as I've already mentioned,
a polite cat.
And so she reached
with a gentle paw
to touch the acorn.
It was smooth
and round
and extremely hard.

"How kind,"
she said.
"Very, very kind.
But my teeth,
you see . . .
my teeth
are sharp and strong,
of course."
And she opened her mouth
to show
just how sharp
and how strong.
"But I'm afraid
they aren't nearly
as sharp and strong
as yours.
I don't believe

I could eat
an acorn,
no matter how hard
I tried."

It was the squirrel's turn
to say,
"Oh!"
She leaned forward
to peer at Patches's teeth.
"I see-see-see,"
she said.
And then she sat for a moment,
thinking
and nibbling on the acorn
herself.
(It would,
after all,
be a shame
to let a perfectly good acorn
go to waste.)

"Have you not found anything
that suits your teeth?"
she asked
after several nibbles.

Patches ducked her head,
embarrassed.
“I did catch a mouse,”
she said,
and she gave the fine white fur
on her chest
a good comb
with her spiky tongue.
“It was a young mouseling.”

“Oh!”
exclaimed the squirrel.
“Well,”
she said,
“that’s good, I’m sure.”
She sat up
and her tail
sat up, too, curled, just at the end.

“I’d almost for-for-forgotten about cats
eating mice.”
But then she leaned forward
and studied Patches
closely.
“And you’re st-st-still hungry?”

Patches ducked her head

even lower.
"I let him go,"
she said
to
the
grass.

"Why?"
cried the squirrel.
"Why did you let him g-g-go
when you
were hungry?"

"Because . . . ,"
Patches whispered.
This conversation
was growing more embarrassing
by the minute!
"Because,"
she said again,
more softly
still,
"the mouseling said,
'Please!'"

For a long moment
the squirrel sat silent.

"I s-s-see,"
she said
finally.
Then she lowered her tail
until it rested
on the grass,
and said,
"It would indeed b-b-be hard
to eat
someone who says,
'P-p-please!'"

"Yes,"
agreed Patches.
"Very hard!"

And then cat and squirrel
sat side by side
beneath the solemn moon,
trying to think.
What was there in all the world
for a cat,
alone in the night,
to eat
besides acorns
that were too hard

and baby mice
who were too polite?

11

The wind,
playing among the dry leaves,
said, "Sh-sh-sh-sh-sh!"
The moon stared and stared
as though
he had no one to look at
except
one calico cat
and a small
red
squirrel.
The night
wrapped itself
softly
around cat and squirrel.
But then Patches remembered.
"That noisy dog
across the street,"
she said.
"He has a bowl of kibble.

He has water, too.
I saw."

"Are you talking about G-G-Gus?"
the squirrel cried.
"The meanest dog in t-t-town?
If you eat his food,
he'll eat you
in a s-s-single g-g-gulp!"

Patches considered
being eaten in a single gulp.
It sounded
like an experience
she would rather avoid.
But still,
her tummy
kept complaining.

Gazing across the street,
she could see
that
lump was
pointy Gus's
a doghouse.
She could make out Gus's bowls

beside the doghouse
too,
because,
as you know,
cats see very well
in the dark.

"Does Gus sleep
in the doghouse?"
she asked.

"No-no-no!"
The squirrel flicked her tail
with each "no!"
"Gus always spends the night
on the b-b-back stoop,
as close
to his b-b-boy
as he can g-g-get."

Patches's tummy rumbled
again.
Something must be done!
She gave her paw
a lick,
drew it across her ginger ear

for luck,
then stepped out
into the street,
            holding
            head
            and
            tail
            high.

Surely
the meanest dog in town
barked so hard during the day
that he must sleep
soundly
at night.

The wind sighed,
and the moon hid his face
behind another cloud.

The squirrel
sat perfectly still,
her paws neatly folded
across her stomach,
watching

the
white
tip
of
Patches's
tail
disappear
in
the
dark.

"Oh my-my-my!"
she whispered.
"I hope that little c-c-cat
is quick!"

12

The first obstacle
Patches encountered
was,
of course,
the fence.
It was tall

and strong
and made of a sturdy metal mesh.
But a fence
perfectly designed
to confine an enormous dog
may present little challenge
for a small cat.
Patches quickly found
a way in.
Gus had been digging
in one corner,
and if she didn't mind
scooching her neat white belly
through some crumbly dirt,
she   yard.
could   Gus's
crawl   into
under   right
the   and
fence

When she emerged,
she looked over at the stoop.
The squirrel had been right.
A Gus-size lump
lay stretched

along it.
Even with her night-seeing eyes,
she couldn't make out
the
long,
limp
ears,
the enormous mouth,
or the yellow teeth,
but she knew
that shape had to be Gus.

Patches
tiptoed
through the grass,
trying
to avoid
the crisp
leaves
scattered
about.

But despite being a cat
with very small paws,
that was a bit
like trying

to walk on air.
So the fallen leaves said,
rustle,
        rustle,
        snapple,
                        crick
with each
and every
step.

Patches tiptoed on.
Gus remained a lump on the stoop.

Patches's tummy rumbled even louder
as she approached Gus's bowl.

Ten   more   inches.
                Six.
        Two.

She leaned
over the edge of the bowl.
She opened her mouth.
She picked up
a crumb of Gus's kibble.

The kibble didn't have
the nice fishy taste
of the kibble served
in the chipped blue bowl.
Still,
it was food,
the first food
Patches had tasted
since breakfast.
And breakfast
had been long, long ago.

But just as the little cat bit down,
just as the taste of kibble
burst
on her small, pink tongue,
just as her tummy
rumbled again,
this time in appreciation
for what was about to come,
just as all that happened,
Patches noticed something.
It was something
so astonishing
that she almost forgot to swallow.

Right in front of her,
under her own pink-and-black nose,
a place.
A special place.
The one she'd been searching for
all along!
This was it
exactly.
Hidden away,
snug,
dark,
quiet,
very, very special.

It was supposed to be a doghouse.
Patches knew that.
It was supposed to be Gus's doghouse.
She knew that,
too.
But it couldn't have been more perfect
or more exactly
what she needed
if it had been built
just
for her.

She sniffed.
The space smelled of Gus.
In fact,
it smelled a whole lot of Gus.
(And you'll remember
that Gus smelled a whole lot!)
But the truth is,
though cats have very good noses—

far better than yours or mine—
their opinions about smells
are different
than ours.
And Patches found
the strong smell of Gus
rather pleasant,
despite the "go away" personality
that went with it.

Indeed,
the fragrance—
for that's what it was to Patches,
a fragrance,
not a bad smell—
reminded her
of the nest of blankets
into which she'd been born.
It reminded her
of sleeping
with her mother
and her sisters
and her brothers,
curled around her.
Of being small
and cared for

and utterly,
completely
safe.

The smell
and the nicely enclosed space
made Patches feel so good,
in fact,
that she quite forgot
about being hungry.

She tiptoed into Gus's house
and lay down
in the deepest,
darkest
corner.
She gave the tip
of
her
tail
a loving lick,
closed her eyes,
and set the motor
of her most contented purr
thrumming.

13

In the still of the night,
Patches woke
suddenly.
Her tummy woke her.
Not the growly rumble of hunger,
though you would expect
by this time
she must have been very hungry
indeed.
It was that other feeling,
the wriggle
she'd been noticing
of late.
But what she felt this time
was more than a wriggle.
It might have been a fist
clenching,
except that the fist was her belly.
In fact,
the fist was her whole body,
drawing tight,
squeezing,
squeezing,
then

finally . . .
letting go.

After a too-brief moment
it happened again.

And then again.

The clenching was so strong
and so entirely new
that it frightened Patches.
What was happening?
She wanted her girl!
She wanted her girl close!
She wanted her girl *now*!
But,
of course,
her girl was nowhere
near.
And the fierce clenching
came again.
"Help!"
Patches cried,
exactly as she had called
to the moon
earlier.

Though this time
it wasn't the moon
she wanted
to come to her rescue.
What could the moon do
for a bellyache?
But surely someone was near.
Anyone.
"Help!"
she called again.
"Please!"

And someone did hear her.

Can you guess who?

It wasn't the moon.
The moon sees everything,
but the truth is,
he hears very little.

And it wasn't the small red squirrel.
The squirrel had watched
Patches disappear
under
Gus's
fence

and then,
afraid to watch any longer,
she had climbed a tree
and tucked herself
away
in her leafy nest.
She hoped to sleep
through the sounds
of a calico cat
being eaten
in a single gulp.

It wasn't Patches's girl,
either,
though the girl
certainly would have come
if she'd only
been able to hear
her cat's call.
But the girl was blocks away
and sound asleep,
a salty crust
of tears
dried on her cheeks.
She had gone to sleep
crying

over her missing
Patches.

No,
the one who heard Patches's call was—
you've guessed it,
haven't you?—
none other than
the
meanest
dog
in
town.

14

Gus lifted his great head
to listen.
The night was still dark,
but there it was again . . . that sound.
He sighed
and dropped his chin
to his paws.
Whoever was calling
had nothing to do

with him.
Truth be told,
no one
had anything
to do with him
these days.
Even his boy
spent little time
out in this green yard
with his dog.
So whoever was making that noise
was none
of his
concern.

"Help!"
The call came again,
and Gus lifted his head
once more.
The voice was so close.
Almost as though the call came
from inside his yard.
Almost as though it came
from inside
his very own
doghouse.

Which wasn't possible,
of course.
Who would dare
go inside
a doghouse
belonging
to the meanest dog in town?

"Please!"
the voice said.
"Can someone come?"

Gus rather liked that word . . .
please.
He couldn't remember
when anyone
had ever
said "Please!" to him.
They said, "NO!"
They said, "SIT!"
And "STAY!"
Even "SHUT UP!"
But never "*Please!*"

Gus tilted his head
to hear better.
"Somebody!"

the voice said again.
And then, "Anybody!"
And then, "Please!"
once more,
though the "Please"
got very small
this time.

Gus leaped to his feet.
He was certainly an *anybody*!
He was,
in fact,
somebody.
He was
even
a rather large somebody.
And whoever was calling
might need
to
be
helped
down
from
a low branch
or bog
dug a
out of

over
lifted some
or obstacle.

If that was the kind of help needed,
a large dog such as he
could surely be useful.

He shook himself awake,
the shake
starting with his head
and
his
long,
limp
ears,
traveling down his back
and ending
with his whiplike tail.

But before he stepped
down into the yard,
he stopped to think.
Maybe
when he got there—
wherever *there* was—

whoever was calling would say,
"Not you!
I didn't mean for *you* to come."
Maybe they would say,
"I don't need help from the meanest dog in town."
Who would?

Gus lay down once more,
rested his head on the concrete stoop,
and closed his eyes.
Some things just weren't his problem.

But then . . . there it was again.
Louder this time.
"Please!"

And this time when Gus lifted his head
he knew . . .
the voice really did come
from his doghouse.

The nerve!
He would have to do something
about that.
Not that he liked his doghouse
all that much.

He much preferred the big house
where his boy lived.
But still,
the doghouse *did* belong to him.
It was
just about
the only thing
in this world
that did.
So . . .
Gus lumbered across the dark yard
and shoved his big head
inside the deeper dark of his doghouse,
a growl
already gathering
in his throat.
Can you imagine the picture that greeted him?

Gus found
the
ugly,
patchy
cat,
the one he had sent away
earlier in the day,
curled into a corner,

as though she owned the place.

"What are you doing in my house?"
he roared,
and he opened his mouth
so wide
that he could have . . .
well,
you know exactly what he could have done.
But he didn't.
Not yet,
anyway.
Which leaves us all waiting
to see
what will happen
next.

15

Patches gazed
at the great gray head
thrust
into her special place.
She gazed
at the huge mouth,

too.
When she'd called for help,
this wasn't exactly
the help she'd had in mind.
Even the moon
would have been
friendlier.
And the squirrel was right.
Gus's mouth *was* big enough
to eat
a small cat like her
in a s-s-single g-g-g-ulp.

But before Patches could think about
how uncomfortable it might be
to be eaten
in a single gulp,
the fist
of her belly
clenched
again.
It clenched so hard
that she could no longer think
about anything at all.
She could only feel
what was happening

inside her.
And now
what was happening
outside her
too!

Because,
when she looked back,
she saw
something emerging
from inside her very own body.
A silvery sac,
shiny,
bumpy,
wiggly with life.
Patches had never seen
anything like it.
Never!
What was she to do?

But that was when
some force took over.
The force came
from
so
deep

inside
that she couldn't even call it
a voice.
It was more an understanding.
A certainty.
And she realized she knew
exactly
what to do.
She began to lick
the silvery sac
with all her might
until her rough tongue
tore it open.
And when the sac tore,
a slippery
black
kitten
slid into the world.
The black kitten had tightly shut eyes
and tightly folded ears.
He had a stubby tail
and the tiniest paws
you could imagine.
He even had
five minuscule claws
on each paw.

And when he opened
his pink mouth,
he cried,
"Mama!"
in a voice so small
it was almost
silence
itself.

Patches,
who was now *Mama*
for the first time in her life,
heard.
And she murmured,
"My baby!"

Then she went back to licking,
licking,
licking.
She licked
her baby's eyes,
his nose,
his ears,
his tail.
She licked her baby
everywhere

until he was soft
and dry.
Then she drew him close
to her belly
to nurse.

But when she looked up,
after all this
had been accomplished,
there he was
still,
the meanest dog in town

with his huge head
not two inches
from her
and her brand-new baby.

Patches didn't know what to say
or do.
She might have tried,
I'm sorry for having my baby in your house.
But she couldn't form the words,
because she wasn't sorry.
Not one little bit.
Gus's house was
the perfect place
for bringing a tiny kitten
into the world.
Besides,
Gus was gazing at her baby
as though at a miracle,
so she said
instead,
"Perhaps you would like
to name him."

"Me?"
Gus whispered

in the smallest voice
ever to emerge
from a large, gray dog.
"You want *me* to name your baby?"

"Of course,"
Patches answered.
"After all,
he was born in your house!"
And without even asking herself
whether it was a wise
thing to do,
Patches gave Gus's great nose
a lick.
Then she waited
to see what he would do.

While she waited,
the moon
slipped
from behind the cloud
that had been hiding his face
and peered down
at them
all.
He was waiting
too.

Gus seemed to have lost
all power of speech.

Now, you and I might think
that a dog who spends his days
up down
running and a fence
shouting,
"GO AWAY!
GO! GO! GO!"
wouldn't have a kitten's name in him,
but we would be wrong.
When Gus finally spoke,
he said,
still in that small voice,
"I think the little fellow
should be called Moonshadow.
Yes . . .
Moonshadow
seems just right."

The moon smiled.
You might not believe me,
but it's true.
The moon really smiled!

16

By this time
the commotion
had awakened the squirrel
in her leafy nest.
She scrambled down
from her tree,
scurried across the street,
and climbed the fence
to see what was happening
to her new friend.
After a moment
she gathered her courage,
jumped down into the yard,
and crept right up next to Gus
so she could peer
into his house.

"Oh!" she said
when she saw the black kitten,
"I see."
And then she added,
"There will be m-m-more,
you know."

"More what?"
Patches asked.

"More b-b-babies,"
the squirrel said.
"When I have b-b-babies,
I always have
m-m-more than one."

"Oh!"
said Patches.
She had a fine imagination—
cats usually do,
just think how they turn
a
    trailing
string
    into
a
    running
mouse—
but she hadn't imagined
even one baby,
let alone more.
Nonetheless,
soon her belly clenched

again,
and when she looked back at the place
that had produced the first kitten,
another silvery sac
was on its way.

By the time
all was done,
two more kittens
lay snuggled
with their mama.
Another boy,
a fine orange tabby.
"His name is Little Thomas,"
Patches said,
suddenly understanding.

And the last,
a tiny calico girl,
all dressed
in ginger and black
patches
on a field of white.

"Perhaps you'd like to name
this one?"

Patches said
to the squirrel.

The squirrel closed her eyes to think.
She had never named
her own babies.
When she opened her eyes
again,
she saw the great gray dog
lying
with his paws stretched
on each side
of mother and babies,
and she said,
"I th-th-think this one should be called
Gus-Gus-Gustina."

"Ah,"
said Patches.
"Gustina it is."

And this time it was Gus
who smiled.
Just about the happiest smile
you've ever seen
on a dog.

Now,
all this sounds
like a happy ending,
doesn't it?
Everyone safe and happy.
Mother and babies.
Gus.
The small red squirrel.
Even the moon.
But our problems
are not quite
over,
which means,
of course,
our story
can't be over
yet.

Because after a while
Patches said,
feeling rather sad
despite the great rush of joy
that had come
with the kittens,
"If only my girl
could see
these fine babies."

"Where is your girl?"
Gus and the squirrel asked
together.
Except that the squirrel said,
"Where is your g-g-girl?"

"I don't know,"
Patches replied.
And then more softly still,
"And she doesn't know
where I am
either."

Gus's long ears
hung
down
even
longer
than
before.
The squirrel's tail
went
    limp and flat.

Patches closed her eyes
and laid her chin

very gently
across her three kittens.
She and her babies
were in trouble,
and she knew it.

17

So . . . here is where our story
has brought us.
We have
not just
one small calico cat,
but a small calico cat
and three tiny,
helpless
kittens,
all far from home.

Gus was perfectly willing
to share his house
and his kibble.
Once he'd seen the kittens,
especially Gustina,
he would have shared anything,
including his heart.

But a house
just right
for a large dog
isn't meant for a cat and kittens,
especially
when the leaves are falling,
which means winter is close.
And besides,
if there is anything
a new mother needs,
it is exactly the right food.
Lots of it.
How else can she make milk
in her own body
for her babies?
And we already know
Patches would not do well
on a diet of polite mouselings.
Gus would have shared his food,
of course,
but his dog kibble
was great chunks,
too big and too dry
for a small cat.

So Patches
and Gus

stayed quiet
for a long time,
thinking.
The silence was broken
finally
by the small red squirrel.
She sat up
and
jerked

attention.

to

tail

her

"You stay p-p-put,"
she said to Patches and Gus.
"I'm going to g-g-go
on the squirrel n-n-network.
There must be
s-s-someone out there
who can help."

"Good," Patches said.
She had no idea
what the squirrel n-n-network was,
but what could she do

except
stay put
anyway?

So the squirrel
ran up the tree
next to Gus's house,
chattering loudly.

"C-c-come!" she called.
"C-c-come squirrels.
C-c-come rabbits.
C-c-come birds and b-b-bats.
We have a mother
who needs our h-h-help!"

And she leaped
from tree   to tree   to tree,
still calling,
until she had disappeared
into the night
and even her voice
had faded away.

When all was silent again,
Gus,

still cradling mother and babies
between his great paws,
spoke.
“You sleep,”
he said to Patches.
“You’ve worked very hard tonight
and must be tired.
I’ll keep watch.”

And so Patches
and the new kittens
slept.
Gus,
faithful to his word,
watched
and
watched
and
watched

through
all
the
rest
of
the
night.

18

At last
the night faded away.
Even the moon
moved on,
dropping
over
the
edge
of
the
earth.

e p
e e
The sun p d

over the other edge.
And a morning breeze
set the dry leaves
gossiping
about all they had seen
during the night,
especially
the new kittens.

Still,
the squirrel
did not return.

Patches woke rested
and nursed her babies,
her put-put-putting purr
quieter this morning.
And Gus continued to watch,
quiet for a change
too.

Even when the mail carriers
pulled up
to the post office
across the street
to begin

sorting the mail,
he didn't shout,
"Go away!
Go! Go! Go!"
even once.

"I wonder what's wrong with Gus?"
one of them said.

But Gus was fine.
Actually,
the big, gray dog was happier
than he'd been
for a long, long time.
You see,
the main ingredient
for happiness—
for dogs
as well as for us humans—
is having someone
to love.
And though he'd only just met her,
Gus *loved* Patches.
And he loved
her three

fine
babies,
one of whom he had named
himself
and one
who was named
after him.

Still . . .
no sign
of the small red squirrel.

19

The sun was riding
high in the sky
by the time Patches and Gus
heard the squirrel
returning.
But it wasn't only
their own squirrel
they heard.
They heard the chatter
of dozens of squirrels,

the soft hop-hop-hopping
of herds of rabbits,
the twittering
of flocks of birds.
And trailing after them all
with its silent,
zigzagging flight,
was even one
very sleepy bat.
(Bats,

as I'm sure you know,
are night creatures.
They fly
through the dark,
then snug in someplace safe
to sleep
through the day.
But this one had heard the call
and had come
anyway.)

All the creatures
gathered around.

"Everyone
has come to h-h-help,"
the squirrel said.
"T-t-tell us
about the girl you have lost."

And so Patches did.
She told them
about her girl,
about the way her girl
petted her
and played with her.
She told them about the sweet scent
of her girl's breath
on the pillow at night.
She even told them
about the chipped
blue bowl
that her girl
filled with delicious kibble
and sometimes even
a touch
of tuna.

"Hmmmm!" said one of the rabbits.
"I've seen lots of girls.
And they live
in lots of different houses.
How will we ever
find a house
by looking
for a girl?"

"Oh!" Patches said.
She hadn't thought
about that.
So then she told them
about
the watching window
and the golden tree
and the leaf
that
    had
wafted
    this
way
    and
that,
the leaf that had called her
from home.

"A golden tree!"
the birds all sang.

"S-s-surely,"
the squirrels chattered,
"we can f-f-find
a golden tree
in front of a h-h-house
with a wa-wa-watching window."

"Yes,"
said the rabbits,
"surely we can."

And so off they flew
and leaped
and hopped
in search of Patches's house.

(The bat
went home
to sleep.
But don't blame him.
If you were a bat
and had been

gobbling mosquitoes
all night long,
you'd surely be sleepy
too.)

Patches helped herself to several bites
of Gus's kibble,
took a long drink of water,
and then,
warmed to the tip of her tail
at having so many good friends,
went back
to caring for her babies . . .
and waiting.

All would soon be well.
She was certain of it.

20

The sun rode low in the sky
by the time the rabbits
returned,
walking steadily and slowly

with only
occasional
an hop.
They flopped to the ground
and said
not a word.

The birds flocked
to the tree
next to Gus's house,
twittering so softly
among themselves
that Patches couldn't make out
a word they were saying.

Then at last,
the small red squirrel arrived
with his friends,
all of them
dragging their tails
like furry rags.

"There are just too-too-too many
houses
and too-too-too many golden trees,"
the squirrel explained,

"and too-too-too many
watching windows, too-too-too.
I'm afraid we will n-n-never
find your house
and your girl."

Patches's
heart
dropped
like
a
stone.

She had been foolish
to leave home
without once
turning
to look back.
She had been foolish
to leave home
at all.

"Oh my,"
she said.
And she gazed
at her tiny babies.

Would she and they
have to make their way
in the world
alone?

And then,
for the first time,
she remembered
someone else.
The mouseling!
The mouseling with
the bright berry
in his mouth.
The same kind of berry
that grew on the bushes
around her house!
She hadn't told her new friends
about the berries.
She hadn't told them
about the mouseling,
either.
Maybe,
just maybe,
the bright red berry
came from *her* bushes.
If so,

surely
the mouseling could help!

And so Patches explained again.
This time not
only
about her girl
and the golden tree
and the watching window.
This time
she explained
about the bushes
filled with bright berries
around the base
of the house.
And about the mouseling
who,
perhaps—
just perhaps—
knew right
where those bushes
grew.

Then,
although it was very hard
for her to leave her kittens,

even for a moment,
she gave each
a lingering lick
and said,
"Gus will watch over my babies
while they sleep.
Why don't I come with you?
We'll find the mouseling,
and together
we'll find my house."

And so squirrels
and rabbits
and birds
and Patches
set off in search
of a mouseling
who surely knew
exactly
where to find
her house.

21

It didn't take long to find
the mouseling.
His nest lay between the roots of the great oak
just behind the post office.
He was tucked in with
his mother
and his brothers and sisters.
The mother mouse

was more than a bit startled
to have a cat
poke her pink-and-black nose
and her long, white whiskers
into her nest.
But the mouseling said,
"It's all right, Mama.
If you only say 'please,'
this cat
won't eat you."

His mother wasn't so sure
about the power
of *please,*
even though
she had faithfully taught
her children
to say it.
But since this cat
already had her nose and whiskers
inside the nest,
she squeaked "p-l-e-a-s-e"
as sweetly as she could,
then stayed very still,
waiting
to see what would happen
next.

But Patches,
as we know,
had no interest in sampling mice.
Instead she explained
about the berry bushes,
about how important it was
to find them
and the house
and the girl,
too.
"The berry!"
the mouseling shouted.
"Oh, that delicious red berry!
Of course,
I can show you
exactly
where I found it."

And Patches
and the flocks of birds
and herds of rabbits
and half the squirrels in town
followed the mouseling
through the grass,
along a sidewalk,
across several streets—
always looking both ways first—

and at last,
to a yard
with a golden tree,
a watching window,
and a whole row
of bushes
with bright berries
stretched all along the base of the house.

Patches had never seen
her house
before,
not from the outside.
But she knew
she had found the right place
the instant she saw it.
Just looking at it
set her fine, white whiskers trembling.
“That’s it!” she cried.
“That’s my golden tree
and my watching window,
too.
It’s where my chipped blue bowl
lives
and my girl.

Especially my girl."

And she ran up to the front door
and mewed
as loudly
as one small calico cat
could,
"I'm here!
I'm here!
I've come home!
At last!"

And the door flew open
and a girl appeared
and gathered Patches
into her arms.
(Our happy ending,
don't you think?)
The girl kissed Patches
and hugged her
and dripped happy tears
on her patchy fur.
"My Patches," she cried.
"My dear, dear Patches!
I knew you'd come home!"
And with that

she stepped back inside the house,
still holding Patches close,
and shut the door.

"I'm going to keep you safe,"
she told her beloved cat.
"You'll never,
ever,
ever
go outside
to get lost
again!"

It should have been a joyous moment—
and it was,
except for one small
problem.
When Patches heard the door
snap shut,
she could think of only
one thing.
Her babies.
Her babies!
Unless she could get
her girl to understand
about her kittens,

she would never
see them
again!

And so she cried,
loud and strong,
"My babies!
We have to go back for my babies!"

But,
of course,
though the girl loved Patches
with all her heart,
she heard only,
"Meow!
Meow, meow, meow, meow!"

"I know,"
she said.
"You're so happy
to be home."

And still holding Patches close,
she went to find
the chipped blue bowl
to give her

an early supper.

A happy ending.

Almost.

22

Outside the house
the squirrels,
the rabbits,
the birds,
and the little mouseling
all
gasped.
Every one of them
had thought
Patches's problems
would be over
when they found her house.
No one had thought
to make a plan
for reuniting
the little mother
with her babies

after they'd found
her girl.

"We'll b-b-break the d-d-door down!"
the squirrels cried.
"We'll peck at the windows!"
the birds chirped.
"We'll hide close by and watch!"
the rabbits whispered.
Because the truth is,
even when rabbits want very much to help,
they
are not
exactly
brave.

"Do it!
Do it!
All of you!"
the mouseling squeaked.
"And while you're doing it,
I'll
scare
the
girl!"

"A l-l-little thing like you?"
the squirrel exclaimed.
"Scare the g-g-girl?"

But the mouseling said only,
"Don't worry.
I know how to scare her.
Just you wait and see!"

And so each of Patches's friends
did what they had proposed.
The squirrels
pelted the door
with acorns.
The birds
flew at the watching window
and pecked it
with their sharp beaks.
The rabbits,
who had promised
only to hide,
if you'll recall,
did much more.
They ran up onto the front porch
and thumped
their back feet

loudly
before they ran
back beneath the bright-berry bushes
to hide.
Then they ran
onto the porch
and thumped
and scurried away
again.

And while all this was going on
the little mouseling waited
quietly
by the front door.
What do you think
is going to happen?

23

Sure enough,
the door flew open,
and the girl,
still holding Patches,
stepped out
onto the stoop

to see
what all the racket
was about.

"Here I come!"
the mouseling squeaked,
and he skittered
up the girl's leg,
scrambled the length
of her arm,
dashed across her shoulder,
and then
scampered right over the top of her head.

After that,
he
scurried
down
the
other
side
almost
as
fast
as
falling.

Now,
let me explain something.
This girl wasn't
really
afraid of mice.
Most people aren't,
if you think about it.
Who lies
in bed
at night
thinking, *MICE!*
and shivering
the way we might
if we knew
a great black bear
was prowling
about?
But if she wasn't afraid,
she was certainly
surprised.
(That's what mice
have going for them,
the surprise trick.)
Because when this girl
stepped out
onto her front porch

to see
what all the commotion was about,
a mouse
was the last thing in the world
she expected
to meet.
And she certainly didn't expect
to have one,
not even a very small mouseling,
run up one side of her body and down the other.

So,
though she wasn't
exactly
frightened,
she certainly was
startled.
Seriously startled.

And what do you do when you're startled?
You jump.
Right?
And if you happen
to be holding something,

even if you're holding something
very, very close,
what else might you do?

It's just possible
    that you might
        throw up your hands
                    and let
                    the something
                    drop.

And that's exactly what this girl did.

Her hands flew into the air
and released Patches.

Just for a second.

But a second was all it took,
because Patches took the chance
and leaped
        out
            of
                her
                    girl's
                        arms!

She landed on her feet,
of course,
because cats are good at landings—
and she took off running.

She headed back
toward
the post office
and Gus's yard
and his doghouse
and Gus himself . . .
and her three
brand-
new
babies.

24

The girl wailed!
She had been so happy
to have Patches back.
And here her little cat was
. . . running
    . . . running
        . . . running away!

"Patches!"
the girl cried.
"Stop!"

Patches heard,
but though she loved her girl,
she paid no attention.
At this moment,
she loved no one more
than Moonshadow
and Little Thomas
and Gustina,
because that's the way it is
with mothers,
even brand-new ones.

"COME BACK!"
the girl called,
running
after.

Patches ran
even faster.

The squirrels,
the birds,
and the rabbits
scattered.
The mouseling,
too.
Now that a human
was involved,
they needed
to be out of the way.
Even the bat
woke
in the comfy attic
where
he
was
hanging
by

his
toes,
listened to the commotion
for a moment,
then
sighed
and
drifted
back
to sleep.

Daytime folks
made so much noise!

As Patches ran,
she kept watch
for the flapping
red, white, and blue flag
in front of the post office
across from Gus's yard.
She was a cat
of the world
now
and knew
about post offices and

f
l
a
p
p
i
n
g
flags.

When she spied it
at last,
she knew
her babies
were near,
all snug and safe
with her friend Gus.

The girl caught up just in time
to see her cat dash
across the street
and duck under
the corner of the fence
right
into Gus's yard.

"Patches! STOP!"
the girl cried.
And then,
when she saw her little cat
heading
straight
for
Gus
and his house,
she added,
"Don't you know?
That's the **meanest** dog in town!"

But Patches didn't stop.
She didn't even slow down.
She just ran right up
to the enormous gray dog
who lay,
half-in,
half-out
of his doghouse,
his chin resting
on his great gray paws.

The girl covered her eyes.
She couldn't bear

to see
what was going to happen
next.

(If you're scared,
you might want
to cover your eyes
too,
though it is rather difficult
to read
that way.)

25

When Patches reached Gus,
she stopped
just inches from his nose.
"I'm back, Gus!"
she cried.
"How are my babies?"
She tried to look past him
into the doghouse,
but he was blocking
the way.

Without raising his chin
from his paws,
Gus replied,
sweetly,
"*My* babies are just fine.
Nice of you to ask."

As I said,
Gus spoke sweetly,
but Patches couldn't help but hear
that word,
the small one
that causes so much trouble
in this world . . .
my.
Patches had said
"*my* babies"—
"How are *my* babies?"—
and Gus had said
"*my* babies"
back.
"*My* babies are just fine."
As though
the babies
they were discussing

belonged
to him!

Patches licked her nose,
once,
twice,
three times.
(You'll remember
that cats always do that
when they are unhappy . . .
or scared . . .
or
just
plain
mad.
And Patches was all three.)
Her fine imagination
was sending up warning signals
all
                    over
the
                    place.

Lots
and lots

and lots
of warning signals.

Patches spoke again,
but more carefully this time.
"Gus,"
she said,
"*where* are the kittens
I left with you?
The ones I asked you to watch over
for just
a
little
while?
Where are *MY* babies?"

"You mean Moonshadow
and Little Thomas
and Gustina?"
Gus asked,
as though there might be
another set of babies
under discussion
here.

"Yes,"
Patches said,

still speaking softly,
carefully.
"I mean
Moonshadow
and Little Thomas
and Gustina."
Just the taste
of the names
on her tongue
made Patches want to howl,
but she kept tight control
and asked again,
softly,
carefully,
"Where are they,
Gus?"

After all,
who knew
what the meanest dog in town
might do
if she made him angry?
Who knew
what he might
already
have done?

"Such nice babies,"
Gus replied,
still without lifting his chin
from his paws.
"I've got them right here.
Warm
as toast."
And he licked
his great gray lips,
as though the place
that kept
the babies warm
might be inside his belly.

The fur stood up
all along Patches's spine.

Her tail p u f f e d , like a bottle brush.

But she tried to stay calm.

"Gus," she said,
using her best mother-voice,
the kind
everyone listens to,

even enormous dogs.
(You know
exactly
the mother-voice I mean.)
"Gus," she said
again.
"I want to see Moonshadow
and Little Thomas
and Gustina . . .
now."

"Certainly,"
Gus replied.
And he lifted his enormous head
so they both could gaze
at the pile
of kittens,
black and orange tabby and calico,
curled into a furry ball
between his paws.
Then he looked into Patches's eyes,
his brown eyes
into her golden ones,

and said again,
this time
in a deep, deep growl,
"MINE!"

26

Now,
you'll remember
I've told you
that Patches,
while grown,
was a small cat.
And you'll remember,
too,
that Gus was a very large dog.
But Patches was also a mother,
and mothers
across the world
have a way about them
when their babies
are threatened.
So Patches didn't think once
about size.
A hiss rose in her throat,

and her claws pressed
beyond the soft pink-and-black pads
of her paws.
She pulled the curving claws in
and let them slip out again,
feeling how sharp they were,
how they could cut,
how they could slash,
how they could tear.
Her fine imagination
could see
an enormous black nose,
the one right in front of her,
for instance,
decorated
with bright-red lines.

But while being a mother
can make a creature
fierce,
it can also make her wise.
Even a small cat.
So Patches tucked the hiss
away
and s l o w l y retracted her claws.
Who knew

what might happen
to her babies
if she hurt Gus?

So she said
very reasonably,
"You know you can't keep them,
Gus."

Gus,
however,
was too busy
licking her babies,
one at a time,
as thoroughly
and lovingly
as a child might lick
a lollipop,
to seem to hear.

"Babies must have milk,"
Patches explained.
"They can't live
without it.
And you have
no
milk."

"I know,"
Gus replied.
And Patches
breathed easier.
He understands,
she told herself.
He'll let the kittens
come home with me,
because
he understands.

But then Gus said,
"That's why you have to stay
too."
And he reached a great gray paw
and laid it on Patches's back,
pressing her
f l a t   t o   t h e   g r a s s .
"MINE!"
he said,
a single, sharp bark.
And he smiled
a huge doggy smile
that showed every one
of his long
yellow
teeth.

27

Through all this,
the girl had been standing
frozen
on the corner
by the post office.
She didn't dare go closer.
She had always been told
to stay away
from the enormous dog
ran and the fence,
who up down chain-link
saying mean things
to everyone who passed by.
Every child in town
had been told
the same thing.

Still,
that didn't mean
she could do
nothing.
So she stood right where she was
and cried, "HELP!
POLICE!

SOMEBODY!"

Now, if you stand
on a busy corner
and cry,
"HELP!
POLICE!
SOMEBODY!"
it's very likely
that somebody will notice.
And somebody did.
Several somebodies,
in fact.

Three mail carriers came running
from the post office.
Two clerks
and four customers came
from the Piggly Wiggly.
Joe,
from Joe's Gas and Grill,
left his gas pumps
and his grill
and came
too.

And the boy
who loved Gus,
though he didn't spend
enough time with him
since he'd been banished
to the yard,
came running out of his house.
With
every
step
he shouted.
"Gus!"
"Bad dog!"
"What are you doing?"
"Let that cat go!"
"Right now!"

Now, Gus had always been fond of his boy,
and he was fond of him still,
but . . .
release Patches?
If he did that,
he would lose her
and the kittens,
too.
Even the one named Gustina.

And he wasn't about to do that!

So he pressed
just a little more firmly
on Patches's back
and narrowed his eyes.
He glared at everyone gathered around:
the mail carriers,
the clerks
and customers
from the Piggly Wiggly,
Joe
from Joe's Gas and Grill.
Gus even glared at his boy
and folded his great gray lips
back from his long yellow teeth.
It was a look everyone understood.
It said,
"Make me!
I DARE YOU!"

28

"HELP!
POLICE!
SOMEBODY!"
the girl kept crying
even after the crowd
had gathered.
Gus ignored her.
He ignored the crowd of mail carriers
and clerks and customers
from the Piggly Wiggly.
He ignored Joe
from Joe's Gas and Grill
and the woman

who had pulled her car
over to the curb
to see what the commotion
was about.

The only one Gus paid attention to
was Patches,
lying flat
beneath his paw.

"Gus," she said again,
in a voice almost as squeezed
as she was.
"You can't do this!"
Though he could,
of course.
Nonetheless,
Gus listened.
He looked closely at Patches,
too.
She didn't just look squeezed.
She looked scared.
Of me? he thought.
Could this dear little cat be afraid of me?

"I'm sorry," he said,
so softly
that no one heard except
the cat beneath his paw.
"All I wanted . . .

the only thing
in all the world I wanted
was for you and your babies
to stay."

And he lifted his great gray paw,
freeing Patches . . .
at last.

She stood
slowly.
First she gave her three-colored coat
a few licks
to put everything
back in place.
Then she looked into Gus's brown eyes
with her golden ones
and said,
"These babies need me,
Gus,
and I need to go home.
So they must
go home
with me!"

Gus's ears went so
f
l
a
t

a
n
d

l
i
m
p
that they touched
beneath his chin.

He didn't argue,
though.
He just rose
s l o w l y.
When he was full on his feet,
the crowd gasped.
Until then
no one but Patches had known

what was hidden
between the great dog's paws.
But there they were,
three tiny, new kittens,
one black,
one orange tabby,
one calico,
curled into a furry pile!
Three kittens
for all the world to see!

"Oh!" the girl cried.
"Oh! Oh! Oh!
Kittens!
My Patches
had
kittens!"

And everyone
who had come
when the girl had called, "HELP!"—
all of them feeling
more courageous now
that the boy was there

to take charge
of the meanest dog in town—
opened the gate
and flowed into the yard.
They gathered close
to see
the perfect wonder
of babies.

Patches,
just to make sure everyone knew
the babies were,
indeed,
hers,
gave each a lick
with her rough, pink tongue.
And to show
not only that they were hers,
but how proud
she was,
she turned on the loudest
mother-motor purr
anyone had ever heard
from such a small cat.

29

The boy stood
with a hand on Gus's collar,
just to make sure,
while the girl gathered
Patches
and her kittens
to take them home.
(One of the mail carriers helped.
She was delivering mail
to the girl's house
anyway,
she said,
and mother and babies

fit comfortably
inside her pouch.)

Gus watched
sadly
as the girl
and the mail carrier,
his cat
and his kittens,
all
disappeared
down the street.
The excitement over,
everyone else left
as well.
The other mail carriers.
The clerks from the Piggly Wiggly.
The customers,
too.
Joe from Joe's Gas and Grill.
Even the woman
who had stopped
to check out
the commotion.
All of them gone.
Only the boy stayed.

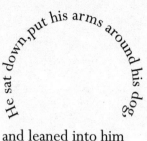

He sat down, put his arms around his dog,
and leaned into him
the way he used to do
when Gus lived
inside the house.

If dogs had been given
the gift
of tears,
Gus would have wept,
but since he had no tears,
he just hung
his great head
and leaned
into his boy.

After a few minutes,
though,
the boy hugged Gus
one last time,
got up from the grass,
and went inside the house.
He had homework waiting.

Later
he brought out a special treat,
hamburger
mixed in with the dry kibble.

But Gus didn't want
a special treat.
He didn't want
dinner at all.
He just wanted Patches
and Moonshadow
and Little Thomas
and Gustina.

When the boy went inside
again,
Gus lifted his great head
and howled.

He was still howling
when Patches
and her kittens
were settled
in a comfy box
in the corner
of the warm kitchen.

He was howling
when the girl
and her mother
and her father
sat down to dinner,
all of them
watching proudly
over their fine cat family.
(As proudly as if
they had been the ones
to bring the kittens
into the world.)

He was howling
when all the town
turned off their lights
and went to bed.

And he was howling
when everyone got up
the next morning,
their eyes heavy
from lack of sleep.

Gus howled
through all of the next day

and into another night.

And then,
a few restless hours
after everyone had climbed
into their beds,
hoping
at last
to sleep,
the howling ceased.
It just stopped mid-howl,
as though someone
had turned off
a switch.

Or as though
the heart
of the great gray dog
had finally shattered.

Few worried
about what might have happened
to Gus,
though.
The entire town
simply sighed

with relief.
The meanest dog in town
was silent . . .
at last.

Only the boy
in the tan house
and the girl
in the house
with the golden tree
and the watching window
(and the row of bright-berry bushes)
sat up in their beds,
suddenly uneasy.
But then,
because they were tired
too,
they lay back down,
each of them,
and went to sleep.

Patches lifted her head
and laid a protective paw
across her babies.
She had grown rather accustomed
to Gus's howl.

She'd found the sound
almost soothing.
At least,
when she heard the great dog's voice,
she knew
exactly where he was . . .
on the corner
across from the post office.
On the corner,
behind a high chain-link fence.
No longer holding her
and her kittens
hostage
with a heavy paw.

Patches tucked her babies in
closer
and lay her chin across her brood.
"Mine,"
she murmured.

She was home,
she reminded herself.
She and her babies were safe.
She had her girl
and her chipped blue bowl

and this warm box
inside her familiar house.

What else could a mother cat
possibly need?

Still . . .
the silence worried her.
What might
an enormous dog
who longed to have her babies
as his own
do
next?

30

Are you worried
too?
Will Gus hurt Patches
and the kittens
if he gets
a chance?
After all,
some folks,

if they can't have what they want,
don't want anyone else
to have it
either.

Or perhaps you are worried
about Gus.
When a dog
has a name,
he doesn't seem
quite so mean
anymore,
does he?
And when you've seen
the way he licked
those kittens—
so gently—
well . . .
maybe we should check
on Gus.
Just to make sure.

Here's what we'll find:
The big gray dog had simply run out of voice
for howling,
so he'd begun prowling the fence

instead.
Silent,
sad,
looking for a way out.
He checked the hole
he'd dug
in the corner.
But a tunnel
just the right size
for a small cat
was no use to him.
And though he tried
to dig
down
deeper,
            he
                    ran
                            into rock
and had to give that up.
He couldn't climb over the top,
either.
One paw got caught in the mesh
when he tried,
and it took him several minutes
to pull it out.
Still

he kept walking
    back
and
    forth
checking
    this
and
    that
until at last
he stopped
at the gate.

Could the solution be so simple?

With all the going
    in
and
    out
recently,
someone had left the latch loose.
Gus stood on his hind legs
and touched it with his nose.
Bump . . . bump . . .

The latch fell away.
A little push

and
the
gate
swung
open.

Gus stepped out
onto the sidewalk.
Free!

Now,
all he had to do was to find
his cat
and his kittens.

But how would he locate them?
He couldn't follow the scent.
Patches and her kittens had been
lifted off the ground
tucked away
in the mail carrier's bag.

Gus sniffed the sidewalk
and found
nothing.
Nothing,

that is,
except . . . one small mouseling.

The mouseling had been so proud
to lead Patches to her home
and so proud
to scare the girl
and get Patches released
again
that when Gus
finally stopped howling,
the mouseling had decided to check.
Perhaps the great gray dog
needed his help
too!

Dog and mouseling
faced each other
on the sidewalk,
and for just a moment
the mouseling considered the possibility
that he might have made a serious
mistake.
Gus was so very BIG!
But then the little mouse gathered his courage
and squeaked,
"Do you want me to show you where they are?"

And,
of course,
Gus wanted exactly that.

So the enormous dog
followed the mouseling through town,
lifting his huge feet
with great care
and setting them down
more carefully
still.
It would never do
to step on a mouseling,
especially one so eager to help.

When they arrived at the house
with the golden tree
and the watching window
and the bright-berry bushes growing
around the base,
the mouseling paused,
and Gus did too.

"Remember,"
the mouseling said,
feeling very solemn
and very grown-up.

"Remember what?"
Gus asked.

"If you only say, 'Please,'
she won't eat you."

Then he helped himself
to another bright-red berry
and scurried home.

What an idea!
Patches eating him!
If dogs could laugh,
that's what Gus would have done.
As it was,
he smiled.
Dogs are very good at smiling!

Then
he
sat
down
on the front porch,
right next to the morning newspaper,
to wait.

31

The instant Patches woke,
she knew.
Gus was at the front door.
Even with the door
tightly shut,
she could smell him.
(I presume you haven't forgotten
about Gus's smell.)
As I've already mentioned,
it wasn't a smell she minded,
except for the fact
that it came with a dog
who had tried to steal
her kittens . . .
and her,
for that matter.
But still,
she did not want the smell—
or the dog who came with it—
in her house.
So though Patches stayed
in her cardboard box,
watching over her kittens,
she kept her golden gaze
on the front door.

Soon her man would get
out of bed
and open the door
to get his newspaper.
And what would Gus do?
Dash inside
and snatch
her kittens
away?

If only she could warn
her humans!

(What a shame
that humans
can't be bothered to learn to understand
cat and dog!
Or squirrel and rabbit and bird,
for that matter.
Whale and wolf,
frog and snake
would be useful
too.
How much gentler
our world could be
if we only knew how to listen
to one another.)

But Patches could do nothing
but wait to see
what would happen,
her heart galloping
in her chest.

And exactly the thing she had feared
took place.
The man opened the front door
without a thought
for what might be waiting
on the other side—
except for his newspaper—

and Gus exploded into the house.

Before anyone could say,
"Oh!"
or
"Help!"
or even
"WHOOPS!"
the enormous gray dog
was dashing through,

his nose scooping up scents
like a vacuum cleaner
sucking dust.

His very fine
sense of smell
took him straight to the kitchen.

He skidded to a stop
in front of the cardboard box
that held Patches
and her kittens
and stood gazing at them all,
his tail wagging fiercely.
(The back-and-forth sweeps
of his whiplike tail
knocked
a pepper grinder,
two place mats,
and a sugar bowl
off the kitchen table,
but he paid no attention.)

Patches leaped to her feet.
Seeing Gus standing over her—
and her babies!—

brought back the memory
of a heavy paw
pressing on her back.
Even worse,
it brought back the moment
when Gus had held her kittens
between his paws
and said,
"MINE!"
So Patches brought out
the only weapons she possessed.
She puffed her tail,
arched her back,
and rumbled a growl in her throat.
G-R-R-R-R-R-R!
Followed by a hiss.
Sha-a-a-a-a!
Her
curving
claws
slipped out of their sheaths.

Gus was amazed,
but,
to be entirely honest,
he was rather amused,
too.

He couldn't think of a single thing to say
to this impressive display
from such a small cat
until he remembered the mouseling's advice.
"Please," he said,
very politely.
"Don't eat me!"

Please!
Don't eat him?
Don't eat this enormous
smelly
dog?

Patches was so astonished
that her back straightened,
her tail unpuffed,
and her
curving
claws
slipped back inside their sheaths.
She found herself looking
straight
into
Gus's
eyes.

She saw no meanness there,
as everyone in town said.
It wasn't even selfishness.
("*Mine*.
These kittens are *mine*!")
Pure and simple,
Patches gazed
into the brown eyes
of a very
lonely
dog.

That was all.

Slowly,
still holding Gus's gaze,
she lay down
and wrapped herself around her kittens.

Gradually,
not looking away,
she found the first put-put-puts
of a purr.
And then,

at last,
she said,
"Hello, Gus."

"Hello, Patches,"
Gus replied.
And then he seemed to remember
that he had not been
the world's best-behaved dog
the last time
they had been together.
His
    tail
        drooped,
his
    head
        drooped,
and
his
long
ears
hung
longer
than
ever.

"I didn't mean . . . ,"
he said.
"Well,
I did *mean*,
I guess,
but . . .
I just wanted . . ."
His apology
dribbled
away.

"You wanted
somebody
to love,"
Patches said,
understanding as mothers do.

In reply,
Gus lay down
right there
on the kitchen floor
and wrapped his great gray body
very tenderly
around the cardboard box,
around the little cat mother
and around her three
tiny
babies.

32

Is this it?
Is this the happy ending
we've been waiting for?
Dog
and cat

and kittens
together,
at last?

But what about the humans
in this story?
Humans have a way
of complicating
happy endings,
especially
those of the animal kind.

And these humans,
the man,
the woman,
the girl,
weren't quite prepared
for an enormous dog,
a smelly one at that,
who seemed
to have taken possession
of their very own cat
and their very own kittens.
Not to mention their very own house.
(You'll note that they,
too,

looked at Patches
and her babies
and said "***MINE***.")

Given the dog's size—
and his long yellow teeth—
they weren't about
to grab him by the collar
and try to haul
him out of their house.
But this was a small town,
and everyone knew
who was attached to the green yard
with the chain-link fence
where Gus
ran up and down
and barked
day and night.
So,
after a brief phone call,
six humans
stood in the kitchen,
looking down
at the box with the cat
and kittens
and at the great gray dog

wrapped around
them all.

The boy spoke first.
“Come on, Gus,”
he said,
and he reached
for Gus’s collar.

Gus growled.
It wasn’t much of a growl.
Just a small one,
deep in his throat.
But it was definitely a growl.

The boy stepped back,
astonished.
His dog had never growled
at him
before!
Never!

“Gus!”
the boy’s father scolded.
And Gus ducked his head,
ashamed.

He hadn't really meant . . .
Well,
he didn't know what he had meant
actually,
except that now he'd found
his cat family,
he couldn't let them
take him
away.

The boy's father stepped up.
He took a firm hold
on Gus's collar
and gave it a tug.
Slowly,
so slowly that the great dog seemed
almost
not to be moving,
Gus
began
to
rise.

But that's when Patches took over.

Before Gus could get

his enormous body
more than two inches
off the floor,
she reached out a paw,
claws delicately extended,
laid it on Gus's leg,
and said,
"MINE!"

Everyone gasped.

"He's mine,"
Patches repeated,
more softly this time,
but she didn't remove her paw
or retract the careful claws
attached to Gus's leg.

Even humans
with no understanding of cat language
couldn't possibly mistake
Patches's meaning.

The boy's dad
released the collar,
and Gus sighed

and sank to the floor.
Once more
he curled himself
around the cardboard box
that held
his cat family.

The humans all began talking at once.
What could they do?
Surely it wouldn't be good
to upset
a new mother!

By the time the humans were quiet again
all was decided:
Gus could stay
as long as Patches
needed him.
The boy could come visit
every day,
take Gus out for walks
or to chase balls in the park.
Perhaps one day
when the kittens were older,
one of them
might even come

to live
with Gus.

Everyone was happy.

But there remained
one small problem . . .
or two,
perhaps.

First,
the smell.
But that was easier to solve
than you might think.

"I have a wading pool,"
the girl said,
"in the backyard.
A little soap,
a little help"—
here she looked at the boy—
"and Gus could smell like roses . . .
or at least like a clean dog."
Everyone liked that idea.
But then the boy's father
looked down at the pepper grinder

and the place mats
and the spilled sugar bowl
on the kitchen floor
and cleared his throat.
"You may find,"
he said,
"that Gus
is a bit,
um,
rambunctious
for a house."

Gus snapped to attention.
Rambunctious?
He wasn't sure what the word meant,
but he knew enough to be offended.
He scrambled
to his feet,
his long ears flapping,
his long tail whacking the wall,
ready to defend
his honor.

For the second time that morning,
though,
Patches took charge.

Once more she laid a paw
with its sharp little claws
on Gus's leg.
"Lie down, Gus,"
she commanded.

Gus lay down.

The humans stared at Patches.
They stared at Gus.
They stared at one another.
Then they laughed.
"I think,"
the girl's father said,
"Patches has Gus
under control."

And she did.

The men,
the women,
the boy,
the girl
returned
to the demands of their day,
and Gus

and Patches
and the kittens
stayed put,
wrapped together
in the warm silence
of the kitchen.

Several quiet moments passed
before Gus opened his brown eyes
and gazed
into Patches's golden ones.
"Do you mind?"
he whispered.
"Is it all right
that I'm here?"

Patches's purr
rumbled to life.
"How could I mind?"
she asked,
and for the second time
she gave his great nose a lick.
"I was searching,
didn't you know?
And I was lucky enough
to find you

and your special place
and your special heart."

Gus wagged his tail . . .
very gently.

And that,
my dears,
is a happy ending.
At last!

Oh . . . and the rest of the animals?
The ones who had cared so much
about mother
and babies
and Gus?
They knew,
in the way animals have
of knowing,
that Gus
and Patches,
Moonshadow
and Little Thomas
and Gustina,
were home safe.
So the grass,

the trees,
the sky,
even a nearby attic
rang with their joy.

And just to add to the celebration,
another
golden
leaf
leaped from the tree
in front of the house
and
fell,
wafting
this way
and
that!